The BOBBSEY TWINS

Freddie and Flossie at the Beach

by Laura Lee Hope

illustrated by Chuck Pyle

Ready-to-Read

Mishawaka-Penn-Harris
Public Library
Mishawaka, Indiana

Visit us at www.abdopub.com

Spotlight, a division of ABDO Publishing Company, is a school and library distributor of high quality reinforced library bound editions.

Library bound edition © 2006

Library of Congress Cataloging-in-Publication Data

Hope, Laura Lee.
Freddie and Flossie at the beach / by Laura Lee Hope; illustrated by Chuck Pyle.—1st ed.
p. cm.—(Ready-to-Read) (Bobbsey twins)
Summary: Twins Freddie and Flossie enjoy a day at the beach with their dog Snap.
1-4169-0268-6 (pbk.)
[1. Twins—Fiction. 2. Brothers and sisters—Fiction. 3. Beaches—Fiction. 4. Dogs—Fiction.]
I. Pyle, Chuck, 1954- ill. II. Title. III. Series.
PZ7.H772Fqc 2005
[E]—dc22 2004017889
1-59961-098-1 (reinforced library bound edition)

All Spotlight books are reinforced library binding and manufactured in the United States of America.

Freddie and Flossie

love the beach.

They splash

in the waves.

Snap splashes too.

Oh, no!

They build a sand castle.

Snap helps.

Oh, no!

15

They play tag.

Snap plays too.

Oh, no!

They rest in the shade.

Snap rests too.

The sun goes down.

Time to go.

Freddie and Flossie
had fun at the beach.

31

Snap did too.